SALOME

Faber Drama

W.H. Auden
Alan Ayckbourn
Peter Barnes
Samuel Beckett
Alan Bennett
Steven Berkoff
Alan Bleasdale
Anne Devlin
T. S. Eliot
Brian Friel
Athol Fugard
Trevor Griffiths
Christopher Hampton
David Hare
Tony Harrison
Vaclav Havel
Sharman Macdonald
Frank McGuinness
Richard Nelson
John Osborne
Harold Pinter
Dennis Potter
Sam Shepard
Tom Stoppard
Timberlake Wertenbaker
Nigel Williams

SALOME

OSCAR WILDE

Translated from the French by
Lord Alfred Douglas

With an Introduction by
STEVEN BERKOFF

Illustrations by Aubrey Beardsley

faber and faber
LONDON · BOSTON

This English translation originally published in 1894
by Elkin Mathews & John Lane, London
This new edition first published with an Introduction in 1989
by Faber and Faber Limited
3 Queen Square London WC1N 3AU

Printed in Great Britain by
Richard Clay Ltd Bungay Suffolk

Introduction © Steven Berkoff, 1989

A CIP record for this book is available from the British Library
ISBN 0-571-14350-4

TO MY FRIEND
LORD ALFRED BRUCE DOUGLAS
THE TRANSLATOR OF
MY PLAY

CONTENTS

INTRODUCTION

by Steven Berkoff

Salome came to me as in a dream – as I read those honeyed words written as if under the heady influence of opium I found myself falling under the spell of Wilde's greatest fairy story. His study in obsession. The concept of the theatre as a temple for our fantasies is here let loose in a torrential rain of language that burns in your mind, a language seldom if ever heard on these shores, although its echoes may be heard just across the waters that divide us. The sounds of Maeterlinck, Flaubert, Baudelaire and Huysmans, an orchestra of language devoted to the senses and to the realization that human beings are a treasure house of both pain and pleasure that must be explored.

Salome was written in the 1890s as the great century was rolling out and venting its last rotting spews and from its ordurous compost grew forth the exotic flowers of the pre-Raphaelites and the curvilinear and sensual lines of the art nouveau. As if racing to complete the *œuvre* before being beached on the virgin shore of the twentieth century, there was a frenzy of activity led by the outsize and over-talented Oscar, around whose feet danced the wicked imp Aubrey Beardsley whose brilliant pen and ink drawings captured the spirit of the time and are nothing less than perfect.

Wilde was obviously influenced by the language of passion and the uncurbed declaration of one's spirit which so readily found a voice in France and so, outrageously he competes with the French poets and writes *Salome* in French, which he offers to his young friend Gide to correct.

Wilde scored the play with great song-bursts of arias, plumes of multi-coloured and ornamental dialogue modelled on 'The Song of Songs'. It naturally found its way into opera which thrives on the grand passion and where great voices need great themes to fuel them, and where we witness the overwhelming turmoil of the spirit. *Salome* was perfect for Strauss and somehow in opera we are allowed to give in to the demands of the flesh which override all moral restraint, whereas in drama the Victorians were a little more circumspect, a little more polite and liked their passion kept down, tied up at the throat with collars and studs and well-corseted, and thus give birth to the comedy of manners in Wilde's four comedies.

ix

ALGERNON: 'Did you hear what I was playing Lane?'

LANE: 'I didn't think it polite to listen sir.'

Meanwhile, *Salome* was considered impolite and banned by the powers of the time to whom all plays had to be submitted, and whose excuse was that biblical figures could not be acted on a stage. A rule not always evoked, but very handy in this particular case and a piece of history in the making with legendary overtones was not to be, and the great French actress Sarah Bernhardt, who had earmarked the title role for herself, packed her bags and went home.

Salome seems to have been a choice vehicle for Wilde to reveal his most personal and deepest feelings for the wonders of erotic love and the sheer delights of the male body. No play reveals Wilde more. It is a cup of the choicest wine and also a rich and poisonous fruit, as if both Salome and Herod are parts of Wilde's character. A kind of Dorian Gray, with Salome his youthful and unfettered lust that must be satisfied, and Herod the obsessive whose whims must be heeded at all cost. The bloated and the beautiful. The language is hypnotic and narcotic as it woos you into oblivion with a lasso of perfumed words spun round your ears. It also reveals the other side of lust, the price that must be paid when lust is satiated, and that is a kind of death of the spirit, and yet who cannot be but moved as Salome keens in a mourning lament while cradling the decapitated head of her 'beloved', the severance of which only served to offer the man's lips without resistance. The apotheosis of greed and desire and the crowning ornament of Wilde's credo 'that nothing succeeds like excess'. We sacrifice everything for one second of ecstasy. How Roman, how simply decadent, darling!

Pure Wilde, a kind of grand folly, an enormous and preposterous gesture. So all these creatures circle each other in a dance of powerful obsessions, whose pivotal centre is the luminous white body of John the Baptist who wants nothing but to fill their ears with their iniquities as he screams their sins to the heavens. Salome dreams of John's lips, and Herod muses and fantasizes on Salome's sweet and succulent body, that he wishes to see move in her dance, and his will must be satisfied since the denial is the proof of some mortality or vulnerability, and those who wish to be gods can be denied nothing. There is no concern, regret or morality involved in their heinous quests, even if Herod offers up half his kingdom for a few languid moments of moving flesh. Only in death does Salome have a taste of regret that 'blood hath a bitter taste but perhaps it is the taste of love'. Herod's orgasmic stream of precious stones are meant to entice Salome from her obsession by tempting another one into her . . . fantasy gems that are powered with alchemical properties. He's really seducing her symbolically, strewing her path with sublimated sex, peacocks and feathers, rubies and onyxes, 'like the eyeballs of a dead woman', I can see Wilde poring over his library book of precious gems and selecting juicily onomatopoeic sounds; chalcedony and chrysoprases. He relentlessly pours out his stream of proffered treasures like an acid-head's dream, a grotesque Pandora's jewel box. He pants his love, offering rows of pearls hung on four rows as if they were calcified spermatozoa. His dried-up shrew of a wife wants some of that passion sloshing out of the vat of Herod's orotund crimsoned lips but she gets nothing. Sterility.

John the Baptist stands in his darkened cistern, his flesh whitened from captivity, tall and thin with skin that Salome describes as 'the roses in the garden of the queen of Arabia are not so white as thy body'. John stands there like a 'column of ivory' atopped with his black hair, 'like a knot of black serpents writhing round thy neck'. Like a giant pale phallus tormenting Salome with the indifference and loathing he has for her worldly and carnal desires while he dreams of another who waits by the sea of Galilee. So into this night-shaded arena under a blood-red moon these creatures weave their dance. Oscar's dance, absurd and gorgeous. It tears away the veil of sobriety or civilized concerns, and allows our fantasies to be paraded before us. It's brave, daring, sexual, and even risks coyness. 'When I pass in my litter beneath the gateway of the idol-sellers, I will let fall for you a little flower, a little green flower.' But even this magnanimous offer from Salome to her love-sick Syrian admirer does not prevent him from killing himself in front of her, a sacrifice she hardly even notices so fixed is she at the time with her new desire.

Either you succumb to this exotic fruit or not, and evidently not in this country since it is rarely performed here even with its great and tempting roles for actors. How strange that on our dark damp shores Wilde's panegyric to the senses never took root.

HOW

I had an opportunity many years ago to study and explore some of the techniques that had been pioneered by Jacques le Coq at his Paris mime school. During that time he worked with the idea of the chorus as a powerful and protean group able to be and reflect whatsoever you wished. A moving centipede of bodies that conveyed atmosphere and emotion and not just a crowd. An articulate core that fed into the environment the very atmosphere of the play. The actor not only has the language of the writer but the body of the performer, and it may be the body is the spiritual part of the whole enterprise since it is unfettered by words and obeys deeper instincts. The body is the unconscious mind at work, while the talking head may be more likened to the engine that sets it in motion. Since according to Wilde's maxim life copies art it was fascinating to witness on an afternoon in Paris a group of street artists using their bodies in a way I had seldom seen used. They were moving very slowly to music and impersonating those slow-motion shoot-outs one sees in Hollywood westerns when the bad guy bites the dust ultra-slow and the blood spurts. The control of their bodies was nothing short of masterly. An utterly disciplined team moving like creatures from another planet, almost weightless in that hot afternoon in the Pompidou centre where you are encouraged to display your art without fear of being curtailed or censored. While I had worked with such effects before in my production of *The Trial* I had not before considered it for a WHOLE production. I decided the weight of Wilde's language had to be carried slowly as if it were a fragile and precious cargo capable of being shattered by anything less than the most careful handling. So I decided to try fusing this movement with the text. It seemed to marry, and the bonding was music, played delicately on a piano.

So I had to find the right style to match Oscar's style, to be a medium for his bejewelled text, and to find the right structure to allow the story to breathe with as little change as possible. So much was the perfume and tapestry in the language that I decided that the stage should be bare and allow the words to bounce off the hard surfaces without being softened or cushioned by 'carpets and ivory tables and the tables of jasper'. These are words that Wilde liked to use but woe betide a designer who seeks to make a table of jasper. Denuded of everything but what was the most vital, and so no wine bottles or glasses, nothing that we could not control or change, nothing whose physical laws were subject to gravity, accident or wilfulness. We would merely act the ingredients of the wine and the fruit so the actors would become language itself.

The Baptist's cistern became a problem, and I felt it was too real; a disembodied voice stuck below stage except for a brief interval of exposure. As life imitates art I knew a camera would crawl slowly down the cistern allowing the audience to set John in his dark, gloomy pit of despair. So we painted a dark square and this was John's murky cistern out of which he would make his laborious ascent to the terrace. The audience thus are always allowed to see him and to imagine that he is there, trapped and confined but we may always gaze at him through the invisible walls. It felt right to set the play in a period close to Oscar's own time, since though the theme was biblical its wit was contemporary. No dialogue need be changed to accommodate this, and the soldiers, Nazarenes, Cappadocians and Syrians, became our party of bright young things, our chorus, our malevolent and amiable chorus, who would be Herod's guests of honour and accomplices. Salome's dance became yet another problem to be dealt with since it is so talked about, and begged for such a mythic image, that who or what could possibly live up to its reputation? What does it mean? Is it a stripping off of all our vanities and pretensions? Is it just a dance? It usually means some erotic striptease where a poor singer or actress bares all and grits her teeth in the alleged name of art. We decided that like everything else it had to be an illusion and that Herod sees her naked fulsome young limbs as the actress 'acts' the dance. The act is the actress's skill, and her body is her own, inviolable and private. Only her Art is ours. And then the question of the 'head' . . . the play seems so beset with problems that I began to understand why few would be bothered to stage it at all. It was more like a short story where the writer allows the reader to fly beyond the limitations of the stage. Like the pit of the Baptist, we decided that Salome should 'create' the head and carry the weight of the monstrous thing in her arms, and react to it and let it be imagined by the audience, rather than have some ugly thing gathering dust on the props table. Thus Salome 'sees' her head and her grief is now more important than the horror of the decapitated head which she kisses. Eventually the words say it all, and we are presenters carrying not the head on a silver salver but the play. We hope that Wilde would approve.

Steven Berkoff, London
September 1989

A NOTE ON "SALOME"

"SALOME" has made the author's name a household word wherever the English language is not spoken. Few English plays have such a peculiar history. Written in French in 1892 it was in full rehearsal by Madame Bernhardt at the Palace Theatre when it was prohibited by the Censor. Oscar Wilde immediately announced his intention of changing his nationality, a characteristic jest, which was only taken seriously, oddly enough, in Ireland. The interference of the Censor has seldom been more popular or more heartily endorsed by English critics. On its publication in book form "Salome" was greeted by a chorus of ridicule, and it may be noted in passing that at least two of the more violent reviews were from the pens of unsuccessful dramatists, while all those whose French never went beyond Ollendorff were glad to find in that venerable school classic an unsuspected asset in their education— a handy missile with which to pelt "Salome" and its author. The correctness of the French was, of course, impugned, although the script had been passed by a distinguished French writer, to whom I have heard the whole work attributed. The *Times,* while depreciating the drama, gave its author credit for a *tour de force,* in being capable of writing a French play for Madame Bernhardt, and this drew from him the following letter:—

The *Times*, Thursday, March 2, 1893, p. 4.

Mr. Oscar Wilde on "SALOME"

To the Editor of The Times.

SIR, *My attention has been drawn to a review of "Salome" which was published in your columns last week. The opinions of English critics on a French work of mine have, of course, little, if any, interest for me. I write simply to ask you to allow me to correct a misstatement that appears in the review in question.*

The fact that the greatest tragic actress of any stage now living saw in my play such beauty that she was anxious to produce it, to take herself the part of the heroine, to lend to the entire poem the glamour of her personality, and to my prose the music of her flute-like voice—this was naturally, and always will be, a source of pride and pleasure to me, and I look forward with delight to seeing Mme. Bernhardt present my play in Paris, that vivid centre of art, where religious dramas are often performed. But my play was in no sense of the words written for this great actress. I have never written a play for any actor or actress, nor shall I ever do so. Such work is for the artisan in literature— not for the artist.

I remain, Sir, your obedient servant,

OSCAR WILDE.

When "Salome" was translated into English by Lord Alfred Douglas, the illustrator, Aubrey Beardsley, shared some of the obloquy heaped on Wilde. It is interesting that he should have found inspiration for his finest work in a play he never admired and by a writer he cordially disliked. The motives are, of course, made to his hand, and never was there a more suitable material for that odd tangent art in which there are no tactile values. The amusing caricatures of Wilde which appear in the *Frontispiece*, "Enter Herodias" and "The Eyes of Herod," are the only pieces of *vraisemblance* in these exquisite designs. The colophon is a real masterpiece and a witty criticism of the play as well.

On the production of "Salome" by the New Stage Club in May, 1905, the dramatic critics again expressed themselves vehemently, vociferating their regrets that the play had been dragged from its obscurity. The *obscure* drama, however, had become for five years past part of the literature of Europe. It is performed regularly or intermittently in Holland, Sweden, Italy, France, and Russia, and it has been translated into every European language, including the Czech. It forms part of the repertoire of the German stage, where it is performed more often than any play by any English writer except Shakespeare. Owing, perhaps, to what I must call its *obscure* popularity in the continental theatres, Dr. Strauss was preparing his remarkable opera at the very moment when there appeared the criticisms to which I refer, and since the production of the opera in Dresden in December, 1905, English musical journalists and correspondents always refer to the work as *founded* on

xvii

Wilde's drama. That is the only way in which they can evade an awkward truth—a palpable contravention to their own wishes and theories. The music, however, has been set to the actual words of "Salome" in Madame Hedwig Lachmann's admirable translation. The words have not been transfigured into ordinary operatic non-sense to suit the score, or the susceptibilities of the English people. I observe that admirers of Dr. Strauss are a little mortified that the great master should have found an occasion for composition in a play which they long ago consigned to oblivion and the shambles of Aubrey Beardsley. Wilde himself, in a rhetorical period, seems to have contemplated the possibility of his prose drama for a musical theme. In "De Profundis" he says: "The refrains, whose recurring motifs make 'Salome' so like a piece of music, and bind it together as a ballad."

He was still incarcerated in 1896, when Mons. Luigne Poë produced the play for the first time at the Théâtre Libre in Paris, with Lina Muntz in the title role. A rather pathetic reference to this occasion occurs in a letter Wilde wrote to me from Reading:—

"Please say how gratified I was at the performance of my play, and have my thanks conveyed to Luigne Poë. It is something that at a time of disgrace and shame I should still be regarded as an artist. I wish I could feel more pleasure, but I seem dead to all emotions except those of anguish and despair. However, please let Luigne Poë know that I am sensible of the honour he has done me. He is a poet himself. Write to me in answer to this, and try and see what Lemaitre, Bauer, and Sarcey said of 'Salome.' "

The bias of personal friendship precludes me from praising or defending "Salome," even if it were necessary to do so. Nothing I might say would add to the reputation of its detractors. Its sources are obvious; particularly Flaubert and Maeterlinck, in whose peculiar and original style it is an essay. A critic, for whom I have a greater regard than many of his contemporaries, says that "Salome" is only a catalogue; but a catalogue can be intensely dramatic, as we know when the performance takes place at Christie's; few plays are more exciting than an auction in King Street when the stars are fighting *for* Sisera.

It has been remarked that Wilde confuses Herod the Great (*Mat.* xi. 1), Herod Antipas (*Mat.* xiv. 3), and Herod Agrippa (*Acts* xiii), but the confusion is intentional, as in mediæval mystery plays Herod is taken for a type, not an historical character, and the criticism is about as valuable as that of people who laboriously point out the anachronisms in Beardsley's designs. With reference to the charge of plagiarism brought against "Salome" and its author, I venture to mention a personal recollection.

Wilde complained to me one day that someone in a well-known novel had stolen an idea of his. I pleaded in defence of the culprit that Wilde himself was a fearless literary thief. "My dear fellow," he said, with his usual drawling emphasis, "when I see a monstrous tulip with *four* wonderful petals in someone else's garden, I am impelled to grow a monstrous tulip with *five* wonderful petals, but that is no reason why someone should grow a tulip with only *three* petals." THAT WAS OSCAR WILDE.

ROBERT ROSS.

Steven Berkoff's production of *Salome* was first staged at the Gate Theatre, Dublin, in 1988. A new production opened at the National Theatre, London, in October 1989.

CHARACTERS

HEROD ANTIPAS, TETRARCH OF JUDÆA
IOKANAAN, THE PROPHET
THE YOUNG SYRIAN, CAPTAIN OF THE GUARD
TIGELLINUS, A YOUNG ROMAN
A CAPPADOCIAN
A NUBIAN
FIRST SOLDIER
SECOND SOLDIER
THE PAGE OF HERODIAS
JEWS, NAZARENES, ETC.
A SLAVE
NAAMAN, THE EXECUTIONER
HERODIAS, WIFE OF THE TETRARCH
SALOME, DAUGHTER OF HERODIAS
THE SLAVES OF SALOME

SALOME

SCENE—*A great terrace in the Palace of Herod, set above the banqueting-hall. Some soldiers are leaning over the balcony. To the right there is a gigantic staircase, to the left, at the back, an old cistern surrounded by a wall of green bronze. The moon is shining very brightly.*

THE YOUNG SYRIAN

How beautiful is the Princess Salome to-night!

THE PAGE OF HERODIAS

Look at the moon. How strange the moon seems! She is like a woman rising from a tomb. She is like a dead woman. One might fancy she was looking for dead things.

THE YOUNG SYRIAN

She has a strange look. She is like a little princess who wears a yellow veil, and whose feet are of silver. She is like a princess who has little white doves for feet. One might fancy she was dancing.

I

THE PAGE OF HERODIAS

She is like a woman who is dead. She moves very slowly.

[*Noise in the banqueting-hall.*]

FIRST SOLDIER

What an uproar! Who are those wild beasts howling?

SECOND SOLDIER

The Jews. They are always like that. They are disputing about their religion.

FIRST SOLDIER

Why do they dispute about their religion?

SECOND SOLDIER

I cannot tell. They are always doing it. The Pharisees, for instance, say that there are angels, and the Sadducees declare that angels do not exist.

FIRST SOLDIER

I think it is ridiculous to dispute about such things.

THE YOUNG SYRIAN

How beautiful is the Princess Salome to-night!

THE PAGE OF HERODIAS

You are always looking at her. You look at

2

her too much. It is dangerous to look at people in such fashion. Something terrible may happen.

THE YOUNG SYRIAN

She is very beautiful to-night.

FIRST SOLDIER

The Tetrarch has a sombre aspect.

SECOND SOLDIER

Yes ; he has a sombre aspect.

FIRST SOLDIER

He is looking at something.

SECOND SOLDIER

He is looking at some one.

FIRST SOLDIER

At whom is he looking ?

SECOND SOLDIER

I cannot tell.

THE YOUNG SYRIAN

How pale the Princess is ! Never have I seen her so pale. She is like the shadow of a white rose in a mirror of silver.

3

THE PAGE OF HERODIAS

You must not look at her.   You look too much at her.

FIRST SOLDIER

Herodias has filled the cup of the Tetrarch.

THE CAPPADOCIAN

Is that the Queen Herodias, she who wears a black mitre sewed with pearls, and whose hair is powdered with blue dust ?

FIRST SOLDIER

Yes ; that is Herodias, the Tetrarch's wife.

SECOND SOLDIER

The Tetrarch is very fond of wine.   He has wine of three sorts.   One which is brought from the Island of Samothrace, and is purple like the cloak of Cæsar.

THE CAPPADOCIAN

I have never seen Cæsar.

SECOND SOLDIER

Another that comes from a town called Cyprus, and is as yellow as gold.

THE CAPPADOCIAN

I love gold.

SECOND SOLDIER

And the third is a wine of Sicily. That wine
is as red as blood.

THE NUBIAN

The gods of my country are very fond of blood.
Twice in the year we sacrifice to them young men
and maidens : fifty young men and a hundred
maidens. But I am afraid that we never give
them quite enough, for they are very harsh to us.

THE CAPPADOCIAN

In my country there are no gods left. The
Romans have driven them out. There are some
who say that they have hidden themselves in the
mountains, but I do not believe it. Three nights I
have been on the mountains seeking them everywhere. I did not find them, and at last I called
them by their names, and they did not come. I
think they are dead.

FIRST SOLDIER

The Jews worship a God that one cannot see.

THE CAPPADOCIAN

I cannot understand that.

FIRST SOLDIER

In fact, they only believe in things that one
cannot see.

THE CAPPADOCIAN

That seems to me altogether ridiculous.

THE VOICE OF IOKANAAN

After me shall come another mightier than I.
I am not worthy so much as to unloose the latchet
of his shoes. When he cometh the solitary places
shall be glad. They shall blossom like the rose.
The eyes of the blind shall see the day, and the
ears of the deaf shall be opened. The sucking
child shall put his hand upon the dragon's lair, he
shall lead the lions by their manes.

SECOND SOLDIER

Make him be silent. He is always saying
ridiculous things.

FIRST SOLDIER

No, no. He is a holy man. He is very gentle,
too. Every day when I give him to eat he thanks
me.

THE CAPPADOCIAN

Who is he?

FIRST SOLDIER

A prophet.

THE CAPPADOCIAN

What is his name?

6

FIRST SOLDIER

Iokanaan.

THE CAPPADOCIAN

Whence comes he?

FIRST SOLDIER

From the desert, where he fed on locusts and
wild honey. He was clothed in camel's hair,
and round his loins he had a leathern belt. He
was very terrible to look upon. A great multitude used to follow him. He even had disciples.

THE CAPPADOCIAN

What is he talking of?

FIRST SOLDIER

We can never tell. Sometimes he says things
that affright one, but it is impossible to understand
what he says.

THE CAPPADOCIAN

May one see him?

FIRST SOLDIER

No. The Tetrarch has forbidden it.

THE YOUNG SYRIAN

The Princess has hidden her face behind her
fan! Her little white hands are fluttering like
doves that fly to their dove-cots. They are like

white butterflies.   They are just like white butterflies.

THE PAGE OF HERODIAS

What is that to you? Why do you look at
her? You must not look at her. . . . Something
terrible may happen.

THE CAPPADOCIAN

[*Pointing to the cistern.*]   What a strange
prison!

SECOND SOLDIER

It is an old cistern.

THE CAPPADOCIAN

An old cistern!   That must be a poisonous
place in which to dwell!

SECOND SOLDIER

Oh no!   For instance, the Tetrarch's brother,
his elder brother, the first husband of Herodias
the Queen, was imprisoned there for twelve years.
It did not kill him.   At the end of the twelve
years he had to be strangled.

THE CAPPADOCIAN

Strangled?   Who dared to do that?

SECOND SOLDIER

[*Pointing to the Executioner, a huge negro.*] That
man yonder, Naaman.

8

THE CAPPADOCIAN

He was not afraid?

SECOND SOLDIER

Oh no! The Tetrarch sent him the ring.

THE CAPPADOCIAN

What ring?

SECOND SOLDIER

The death ring. So he was not afraid.

THE CAPPADOCIAN

Yet it is a terrible thing to strangle a king.

FIRST SOLDIER

Why? Kings have but one neck, like other folk.

THE CAPPADOCIAN

I think it terrible.

THE YOUNG SYRIAN

The Princess is getting up! She is leaving the table! She looks very troubled. Ah, she is coming this way. Yes, she is coming towards us. How pale she is! Never have I seen her so pale.

THE PAGE OF HERODIAS

Do not look at her. I pray you not to look at her.

9

THE YOUNG SYRIAN

She is like a dove that has strayed. . . . She is
like a narcissus trembling in the wind. . . . She
is like a silver flower.

[*Enter Salome.*]

SALOME

I will not stay. I cannot stay. Why does the
Tetrarch look at me all the while with his mole's
eyes under his shaking eyelids? It is strange
that the husband of my mother looks at me like
that. I know not what it means. Of a truth I
know it too well.

THE YOUNG SYRIAN

You have left the feast, Princess?

SALOME

How sweet is the air here! I can breathe
here! Within there are Jews from Jerusalem
who are tearing each other in pieces over their
foolish ceremonies, and barbarians who drink and
drink and spill their wine on the pavement, and
Greeks from Smyrna with painted eyes and painted
cheeks, and frizzed hair curled in columns, and
Egyptians silent and subtle, with long nails of
jade and russet cloaks, and Romans brutal and
coarse, with their uncouth jargon. Ah! how I
loathe the Romans! They are rough and common,
and they give themselves the airs of noble lords.

THE YOUNG SYRIAN

Will you be seated, Princess.

THE PAGE OF HERODIAS

Why do you speak to her? Oh! something terrible will happen. Why do you look at her?

SALOME

How good to see the moon! She is like a little piece of money, a little silver flower. She is cold and chaste. I am sure she is a virgin. She has the beauty of a virgin. Yes, she is a virgin. She has never defiled herself. She has never abandoned herself to men, like the other goddesses.

THE VOICE OF IOKANAAN

Behold! the Lord hath come. The Son of Man is at hand. The centaurs have hidden themselves in the rivers, and the nymphs have left the rivers, and are lying beneath the leaves in the forests.

SALOME

Who was that who cried out?

SECOND SOLDIER

The prophet, Princess.

SALOME

Ah, the prophet! He of whom the Tetrarch is afraid?

SECOND SOLDIER

We know nothing of that, Princess. It was the prophet Iokanaan who cried out.

THE YOUNG SYRIAN

Is it your pleasure that I bid them bring your litter, Princess? The night is fair in the garden.

SALOME

He says terrible things about my mother, does he not?

SECOND SOLDIER

We never understand what he says, Princess.

SALOME

Yes; he says terrible things about her.

[*Enter a Slave.*]

THE SLAVE

Princess, the Tetrarch prays you to return to the feast.

SALOME

I will not return.

THE YOUNG SYRIAN

Pardon me, Princess, but if you return not some misfortune may happen.

SALOME

Is he an old man, this prophet?

THE YOUNG SYRIAN

Princess, it were better to return. Suffer me to lead you in.

SALOME

This prophet . . . is he an old man?

FIRST SOLDIER

No, Princess, he is quite young.

SECOND SOLDIER

One cannot be sure. There are those who say that he is Elias.

SALOME

Who is Elias?

SECOND SOLDIER

A prophet of this country in bygone days, Princess.

THE SLAVE

What answer may I give the Tetrarch from the Princess?

THE VOICE OF IOKANAAN

Rejoice not, O land of Palestine, because the rod of him who smote thee is broken. For from the seed of the serpent shall come a basilisk, and that which is born of it shall devour the birds.

13

SALOME

What a strange voice! I would speak with him.

FIRST SOLDIER

I fear it may not be, Princess. The Tetrarch does not suffer any one to speak with him. He has even forbidden the high priest to speak with him.

SALOME

I desire to speak with him.

FIRST SOLDIER

It is impossible, Princess.

SALOME

I will speak with him.

THE YOUNG SYRIAN

Would it not be better to return to the banquet?

SALOME

Bring forth this prophet.

[*Exit the Slave.*]

FIRST SOLDIER

We dare not, Princess.

SALOME

[*Approaching the cistern and looking down into*

14

it.] How black it is, down there! It must be terrible to be in so black a hole! It is like a tomb. . . . [*To the soldiers.*] Did you not hear me? Bring out the prophet. I would look on him.

SECOND SOLDIER

Princess, I beg you, do not require this of us.

SALOME

You are making me wait upon your pleasure.

FIRST SOLDIER

Princess, our lives belong to you, but we cannot do what you have asked of us. And indeed, it is not of us that you should ask this thing.

SALOME

[*Looking at the young Syrian.*] Ah!

THE PAGE OF HERODIAS

Oh! what is going to happen? I am sure that something terrible will happen.

SALOME

[*Going up to the young Syrian.*] Thou wilt do this thing for me, wilt thou not, Narraboth? Thou wilt do this thing for me. I have ever been kind towards thee. Thou wilt do it for me. I would but look at him, this strange prophet. Men have talked so much of him. Often I have heard the Tetrarch talk of him. I think he is afraid of

15

him, the Tetrarch. Art thou, even thou, also
afraid of him, Narraboth?

THE YOUNG SYRIAN

I fear him not, Princess; there is no man I fear.
But the Tetrarch has formally forbidden that any
man should raise the cover of this well.

SALOME

Thou wilt do this thing for me, Narraboth, and
to-morrow when I pass in my litter beneath the
gateway of the idol-sellers I will let fall for thee a
little flower, a little green flower.

THE YOUNG SYRIAN

Princess, I cannot, I cannot.

SALOME

[*Smiling.*] Thou wilt do this thing for me,
Narraboth. Thou knowest that thou wilt do this
thing for me. And on the morrow when I shall
pass in my litter by the bridge of the idol-buyers,
I will look at thee through the muslin veils, I will
look at thee, Narraboth, it may be I will smile at
thee. Look at me, Narraboth, look at me. Ah!
thou knowest that thou wilt do what I ask of
thee. Thou knowest it. . . . I know that thou
wilt do this thing.

THE YOUNG SYRIAN

[*Signing to the third Soldier.*] Let the prophet

come forth. . . . The Princess Salome desires to see him.

SALOME

Ah!

THE PAGE OF HERODIAS

Oh! How strange the moon looks! Like the hand of a dead woman who is seeking to cover herself with a shroud.

THE YOUNG SYRIAN

She has a strange aspect! She is like a little princess, whose eyes are eyes of amber. Through the clouds of muslin she is smiling like a little princess. [*The prophet comes out of the cistern. Salome looks at him and steps slowly back.*]

IOKANAAN

Where is he whose cup of abominations is now full? Where is he, who in a robe of silver shall one day die in the face of all the people? Bid him come forth, that he may hear the voice of him who hath cried in the waste places and in the houses of kings.

SALOME

Of whom is he speaking?

THE YOUNG SYRIAN

No one can tell, Princess.

17

IOKANAAN

Where is she who saw the images of men painted on the walls, even the images of the Chaldæans painted with colours, and gave herself up unto the lust of her eyes, and sent ambassadors into the land of Chaldæa?

SALOME

It is of my mother that he is speaking.

THE YOUNG SYRIAN

Oh no, Princess.

SALOME

Yes: it is of my mother that he is speaking.

IOKANAAN

Where is she who gave herself unto the Captains of Assyria, who have baldricks on their loins, and crowns of many colours on their heads? Where is she who hath given herself to the young men of the Egyptians, who are clothed in fine linen and hyacinth, whose shields are of gold, whose helmets are of silver, whose bodies are mighty? Go, bid her rise up from the bed of her abominations, from the bed of her incestuousness, that she may hear the words of him who prepareth the way of the Lord, that she may repent her of her iniquities. Though she will not repent, but will stick fast in her abominations, go bid her come, for the fan of the Lord is in His hand.

SALOME

Ah, but he is terrible, he is terrible !

THE YOUNG SYRIAN

Do not stay here, Princess, I beseech you.

SALOME

It is his eyes above all that are terrible. They
are like black holes burned by torches in a
tapestry of Tyre. They are like the black caverns
where the dragons live, the black caverns of Egypt
in which the dragons make their lairs. They are
like black lakes troubled by fantastic moons. . . .
Do you think he will speak again ?

THE YOUNG SYRIAN

Do not stay here, Princess. I pray you do
not stay here.

SALOME

How wasted he is ! He is like a thin ivory
statue. He is like an image of silver. I am sure
he is chaste, as the moon is. He is like a moon-
beam, like a shaft of silver. His flesh must be very
cold, cold as ivory. . . . I would look closer at him.

THE YOUNG SYRIAN

No, no, Princess !

SALOME

I must look at him closer.

THE YOUNG SYRIAN

Princess! Princess!

IOKANAAN

Who is this woman who is looking at me? I
will not have her look at me. Wherefore doth
she look at me, with her golden eyes, under her
gilded eyelids? I know not who she is. I do
not desire to know who she is. Bid her begone.
It is not to her that I would speak.

SALOME

I am Salome, daughter of Herodias, Princess of
Judæa.

IOKANAAN

Back! daughter of Babylon! Come not near
the chosen of the Lord. Thy mother hath filled
the earth with the wine of her iniquities, and the
cry of her sinning hath come up even to the ears
of God.

SALOME

Speak again, Iokanaan. Thy voice is as music
to mine ear.

THE YOUNG SYRIAN

Princess! Princess! Princess!

SALOME

Speak again! Speak again, Iokanaan, and tell
me what I must do.

IOKANAAN

Daughter of Sodom, come not near me! But cover thy face with a veil, and scatter ashes upon thine head, and get thee to the desert, and seek out the Son of Man.

SALOME

Who is he, the Son of Man? Is he as beautiful as thou art, Iokanaan?

IOKANAAN

Get thee behind me! I hear in the palace the beating of the wings of the angel of death.

THE YOUNG SYRIAN

Princess, I beseech thee to go within.

IOKANAAN

Angel of the Lord God, what dost thou here with thy sword? Whom seekest thou in this palace? The day of him who shall die in a robe of silver has not yet come.

SALOME

Iokanaan!

IOKANAAN

Who speaketh?

SALOME

I am amorous of thy body, Iokanaan! Thy body is white, like the lilies of a field that the mower hath never mowed. Thy body is white like the snows that lie on the mountains of Judæa, and come down into the valleys. The roses in the garden of the Queen of Arabia are not so white as thy body. Neither the roses of the garden of the Queen of Arabia, the garden of spices of the Queen of Arabia, nor the feet of the dawn when they light on the leaves, nor the breast of the moon when she lies on the breast of the sea. . . . There is nothing in the world so white as thy body. Suffer me to touch thy body.

IOKANAAN

Back! daughter of Babylon! By woman came evil into the world. Speak not to me. I will not listen to thee. I listen but to the voice of the Lord God.

SALOME

Thy body is hideous. It is like the body of a leper. It is like a plastered wall, where vipers have crawled; like a plastered wall where the scorpions have made their nest. It is like a whited sepulchre, full of loathsome things. It is horrible, thy body is horrible. It is of thy hair that I am enamoured, Iokanaan. Thy hair is like clusters of grapes, like the clusters of black grapes that hang from the vine-trees of Edom in the land of the Edomites. Thy hair is like the cedars of Lebanon, like the great cedars of Lebanon that give their shade to the lions and to the robbers who would hide them by day. The long black

22

nights, when the moon hides her face, when the stars are afraid, are not so black as thy hair. The silence that dwells in the forest is not so black. There is nothing in the world that is so black as thy hair. . . . Suffer me to touch thy hair.

IOKANAAN

Back, daughter of Sodom ! Touch me not. Profane not the temple of the Lord God.

SALOME

Thy hair is horrible. It is covered with mire and dust. It is like a crown of thorns placed on thy head. It is like a knot of serpents coiled round thy neck. I love not thy hair. . . . It is thy mouth that I desire, Iokanaan. Thy mouth is like a band of scarlet on a tower of ivory. It is like a pomegranate cut in twain with a knife of ivory. The pomegranate flowers that blossom in the gardens of Tyre, and are redder than roses, are not so red. The red blasts of trumpets that herald the approach of kings, and make afraid the enemy, are not so red. Thy mouth is redder than the feet of those who tread the wine in the wine-press. It is redder than the feet of the doves who inhabit the temples and are fed by the priests. It is redder than the feet of him who cometh from a forest where he hath slain a lion, and seen gilded tigers. Thy mouth is like a branch of coral that fishers have found in the twilight of the sea, the coral that they keep for the kings ! . . . It is like the vermilion that the Moabites find in the mines of Moab, the vermilion that the kings take from them. It is like the bow of the King of the Persians, that is painted with vermilion, and is tipped with coral. There is nothing in the world so red as thy mouth. . . . Suffer me to kiss thy mouth.

IOKANAAN

Never! daughter of Babylon! Daughter of Sodom! never!

SALOME

I will kiss thy mouth, Iokanaan. I will kiss thy mouth.

THE YOUNG SYRIAN

Princess, Princess, thou who art like a garden of myrrh, thou who art the dove of all doves, look not at this man, look not at him! Do not speak such words to him. I cannot endure it. . . . Princess, do not speak these things.

SALOME

I will kiss thy mouth, Iokanaan.

THE YOUNG SYRIAN

Ah! [*He kills himself, and falls between Salome and Iokanaan.*]

THE PAGE OF HERODIAS

The young Syrian has slain himself! The

young captain has slain himself! He has slain himself who was my friend! I gave him a little box of perfumes and ear-rings wrought in silver, and now he has killed himself! Ah, did he not say that some misfortune would happen? I, too, said it, and it has come to pass. Well I knew that the moon was seeking a dead thing, but I knew not that it was he whom she sought. Ah! why did I not hide him from the moon? If I had hidden him in a cavern she would not have seen him.

FIRST SOLDIER

Princess, the young captain has just slain himself.

SALOME

Suffer me to kiss thy mouth, Iokanaan.

IOKANAAN

Art thou not afraid, daughter of Herodias? Did I not tell thee that I had heard in the palace the beating of the wings of the angel of death, and hath he not come, the angel of death?

SALOME

Suffer me to kiss thy mouth.

IOKANAAN

Daughter of adultery, there is but one who can save thee. It is He of whom I spake. Go seek Him. He is in a boat on the sea of Galilee, and

25

He talketh with His disciples. Kneel down on the shore of the sea, and call unto Him by His name. When He cometh to thee, and to all who call on Him He cometh, bow thyself at His feet and ask of Him the remission of thy sins.

SALOME

Suffer me to kiss thy mouth.

IOKANAAN

Cursed be thou! daughter of an incestuous mother, be thou accursed!

SALOME

I will kiss thy mouth, Iokanaan.

IOKANAAN

I will not look at thee. Thou art accursed, Salome, thou art accursed. [*He goes down into the cistern.*]

SALOME

I will kiss thy mouth, Iokanaan; I will kiss thy mouth.

FIRST SOLDIER

We must bear away the body to another place. The Tetrarch does not care to see dead bodies, save the bodies of those whom he himself has slain.

THE PAGE OF HERODIAS

He was my brother, and nearer to me than a

brother. I gave him a little box full of perfumes, and a ring of agate that he wore always on his hand. In the evening we were wont to walk by the river, and among the almond-trees, and he used to tell me of the things of his country. He spake ever very low. The sound of his voice was like the sound of the flute, of one who playeth upon the flute. Also he had much joy to gaze at himself in the river. I used to reproach him for that.

SECOND SOLDIER

You are right ; we must hide the body. The Tetrarch must not see it.

FIRST SOLDIER

The Tetrarch will not come to this place. He never comes on the terrace. He is too much afraid of the prophet.

[*Enter Herod, Herodias, and all the Court.*]

HEROD

Where is Salome? Where is the Princess? Why did she not return to the banquet as I commanded her? Ah! there she is!

HERODIAS

You must not look at her! You are always looking at her!

HEROD

The moon has a strange look to-night. Has

27

she not a strange look? She is like a mad
woman, a mad woman who is seeking everywhere
for lovers. She is naked too. She is quite naked.
The clouds are seeking to clothe her nakedness,
but she will not let them. She shows herself
naked in the sky. She reels through the clouds
like a drunken woman. . . . I am sure she is
looking for lovers. Does she not reel like a
drunken woman? She is like a mad woman, is
she not?

HERODIAS

No; the moon is like the moon, that is all.
Let us go within. . . . We have nothing to do
here.

HEROD

I will stay here! Manasseh, lay carpets there.
Light torches. Bring forth the ivory tables, and
the tables of jasper. The air here is sweet. I
will drink more wine with my guests. We must
show all honours to the ambassadors of Cæsar.

HERODIAS

It is not because of them that you remain.

HEROD

Yes; the air is very sweet. Come, Herodias,
our guests await us. Ah! I have slipped! I
have slipped in blood! It is an ill omen. It is
a very ill omen. Wherefore is there blood here?
. . . and this body, what does this body here?

28

Think you I am like the King of Egypt, who
gives no feast to his guests but that he shows
them a corpse? Whose is it? I will not look
on it.

FIRST SOLDIER

It is our captain, sire. It is the young Syrian
whom you made captain of the guard but three
days gone.

HEROD

I issued no order that he should be slain.

SECOND SOLDIER

He slew himself, sire.

HEROD

For what reason? I had made him captain of
my guard!

SECOND SOLDIER

We do not know, sire. But with his own hand
he slew himself.

HEROD

That seems strange to me. I had thought it was
but the Roman philosophers who slew themselves.
Is it not true, Tigellinus, that the philosophers at
Rome slay themselves?

TIGELLINUS

There be some who slay themselves, sire. They
are the Stoics. The Stoics are people of no culti-

vation. They are ridiculous people. I myself regard them as being perfectly ridiculous.

HEROD

I also. It is ridiculous to kill one's-self.

TIGELLINUS

Everybody at Rome laughs at them. The Emperor has written a satire against them. It is recited everywhere.

HEROD

Ah! he has written a satire against them? Cæsar is wonderful. He can do everything. . . . It is strange that the young Syrian has slain himself. I am sorry he has slain himself. I am very sorry. For he was fair to look upon. He was even very fair. He had very languorous eyes. I remember that I saw that he looked languorously at Salome. Truly, I thought he looked too much at her.

HERODIAS

There are others who look too much at her.

HEROD

His father was a king. I drave him from his kingdom. And of his mother, who was a queen, you made a slave, Herodias. So he was here as my guest, as it were, and for that reason I made him my captain. I am sorry he is dead. Ho! why have you left the body here? It must be taken to some other place. I will not look at it,—away with it!

[*They take away the body.*] It is cold here. There is a wind blowing. Is there not a wind blowing?

HERODIAS

No ; there is no wind.

HEROD

I tell you there is a wind that blows. . . . And I hear in the air something that is like the beating of wings, like the beating of vast wings. Do you not hear it?

HERODIAS

I hear nothing.

HEROD

I hear it no longer. But I heard it. It was the blowing of the wind. It has passed away. But no, I hear it again. Do you not hear it? It is just like a beating of wings.

HERODIAS

I tell you there is nothing. You are ill. Let us go within.

HEROD

I am not ill. It is your daughter who is sick to death. Never have I seen her so pale.

HERODIAS

I have told you not to look at her.

31

HEROD

Pour me forth wine. [*Wine is brought.*] Salome, come drink a little wine with me. I have here a wine that is exquisite. Cæsar himself sent it me. Dip into it thy little red lips, that I may drain the cup.

SALOME

I am not thirsty, Tetrarch.

HEROD

You hear how she answers me, this daughter of yours?

HERODIAS

She does right. Why are you always gazing at her?

HEROD

Bring me ripe fruits. [*Fruits are brought.*] Salome, come and eat fruits with me. I love to see in a fruit the mark of thy little teeth. Bite but a little of this fruit, that I may eat what is left.

SALOME

I am not hungry, Tetrarch.

HEROD

[*To Herodias.*] You see how you have brought up this daughter of yours.

HERODIAS

My daughter and I come of a royal race. As

for thee, thy father was a camel driver! He was
a thief and a robber to boot!

HEROD

Thou liest!

HERODIAS

Thou knowest well that it is true.

HEROD

Salome, come and sit next to me. I will give
thee the throne of thy mother.

SALOME

I am not tired, Tetrarch.

HERODIAS

You see in what regard she holds you.

HEROD

Bring me——What is it that I desire? I
forget. Ah! ah! I remember.

THE VOICE OF IOKANAAN

Behold the time is come! That which I fore-
told has come to pass. The day that I spake of
is at hand.

HERODIAS

Bid him be silent. I will not listen to his voice.
This man is for ever hurling insults against me.

HEROD

He has said nothing against you. Besides, he
is a very great prophet.

HERODIAS

I do not believe in prophets. Can a man tell
what will come to pass? No man knows it. Also
he is for ever insulting me. But I think you are
afraid of him. . . . I know well that you are afraid
of him.

HEROD

I am not afraid of him. I am afraid of no man.

HERODIAS

I tell you you are afraid of him. If you are not
afraid of him why do you not deliver him to
the Jews who for these six months past have been
clamouring for him?

A JEW

Truly, my lord, it were better to deliver him
into our hands.

HEROD

Enough on this subject. I have already given
you my answer. I will not deliver him into your
hands. He is a holy man. He is a man who has
seen God.

A JEW

That cannot be. There is no man who hath seen
God since the prophet Elias. He is the last man

who saw God face to face. · In these days God doth not show Himself. God hideth Himself. Therefore great evils have come upon the land.

ANOTHER JEW

Verily, no man knoweth if Elias the prophet did indeed see God. Peradventure it was but the shadow of God that he saw.

A THIRD JEW

God is at no time hidden. He showeth Himself at all times and in all places. God is in what is evil even as He is in what is good.

A FOURTH JEW

Thou shouldst not say that. It is a very dangerous doctrine. It is a doctrine that cometh from Alexandria, where men teach the philosophy of the Greeks. And the Greeks are Gentiles. They are not even circumcised.

A FIFTH JEW

No man can tell how God worketh. His ways are very dark. It may be that the things which we call evil are good, and that the things which we call good are evil. There is no knowledge of anything. We can but bow our heads to His will, for God is very strong. He breaketh in pieces the strong together with the weak, for He regardeth not any man.

FIRST JEW

Thou speakest truly. Verily, God is terrible.

35

He breaketh in pieces the strong and the weak
as men break corn in a mortar. But as for this
man, he hath never seen God. No man hath
seen God since the prophet Elias.

HERODIAS

Make them be silent. They weary me.

HEROD

But I have heard it said that Iokanaan is in
very truth your prophet Elias.

THE JEW

That cannot be. It is more than three hundred
years since the days of the prophet Elias.

HEROD

There be some who say that this man is Elias
the prophet.

A NAZARENE

I am sure that he is Elias the prophet.

THE JEW

Nay, but he is not Elias the prophet.

THE VOICE OF IOKANAAN

Behold the day is at hand, the day of the Lord,
and I hear upon the mountains the feet of Him
who shall be the Saviour of the world.

HEROD

What does that mean? The Saviour of the world?

TIGELLINUS

It is a title that Cæsar adopts.

HEROD

But Cæsar is not coming into Judæa. Only yesterday I received letters from Rome. They contained nothing concerning this matter. And you, Tigellinus, who were at Rome during the winter, you heard nothing concerning this matter, did you?

TIGELLINUS

Sire, I heard nothing concerning the matter. I was but explaining the title. It is one of Cæsar's titles.

HEROD

But Cæsar cannot come. He is too gouty. They say that his feet are like the feet of an elephant. Also there are reasons of state. He who leaves Rome loses Rome. He will not come. Howbeit, Cæsar is lord, he will come if such be his pleasure. Nevertheless, I think he will not come.

FIRST NAZARENE

It was not concerning Cæsar that the prophet spake these words, sire.

HEROD

How?—it was not concerning Cæsar?

FIRST NAZARENE

No, my lord.

HEROD

Concerning whom then did he speak?

FIRST NAZARENE

Concerning Messias, who hath come.

A JEW

Messias hath not come.

FIRST NAZARENE

He hath come, and everywhere He worketh miracles!

HERODIAS

Ho! ho! miracles! I do not believe in miracles. I have seen too many. [*To the Page.*] My fan.

FIRST NAZARENE

This Man worketh true miracles. Thus, at a marriage which took place in a little town of Galilee, a town of some importance, He changed water into wine. Certain persons who were present related it to me. Also He healed two lepers that

38

were seated before the Gate of Capernaum simply by touching them.

SECOND NAZARENE

Nay; it was two blind men that He healed at Capernaum.

FIRST NAZARENE

Nay; they were lepers. But He hath healed blind people also, and He was seen on a mountain talking with angels.

A SADDUCEE

Angels do not exist.

A PHARISEE

Angels exist, but I do not believe that this Man has talked with them.

FIRST NAZARENE

He was seen by a great multitude of people talking with angels.

HERODIAS

How these men weary me! They are ridiculous! They are altogether ridiculous! [*To the Page.*] Well! my fan? [*The Page gives her the fan.*] You have a dreamer's look. You must not dream. It is only sick people who dream. [*She strikes the Page with her fan.*]

SECOND NAZARENE

There is also the miracle of the daughter of Jairus.

FIRST NAZARENE

Yea, that is sure.　No man can gainsay it.

HERODIAS

Those men are mad.　They have looked too long on the moon.　Command them to be silent.

HEROD

What is this miracle of the daughter of Jairus?

FIRST NAZARENE

The daughter of Jairus was dead.　This Man raised her from the dead.

HEROD

How! He raises people from the dead?

FIRST NAZARENE

Yea, sire ; He raiseth the dead.

HEROD

I do not wish Him to do that.　I forbid Him to do that.　I suffer no man to raise the dead. This Man must be found and told that I forbid Him to raise the dead.　Where is this Man at present?

40

SECOND NAZARENE

He is in every place, my lord, but it is hard to find Him.

FIRST NAZARENE

It is said that He is now in Samaria.

A JEW

It is easy to see that this is not Messias, if He is in Samaria. It is not to the Samaritans that Messias shall come. The Samaritans are accursed. They bring no offerings to the Temple.

SECOND NAZARENE

He left Samaria a few days since. I think that at the present moment He is in the neighbour-hood of Jerusalem.

FIRST NAZARENE

No ; He is not there. I have just come from Jerusalem. For two months they have had no tidings of Him.

HEROD

No matter! But let them find Him, and tell Him, thus saith Herod the King, ' I will not suffer Thee to raise the dead.' To change water into wine, to heal the lepers and the blind. . . . He may do these things if He will. I say nothing against these things. In truth I hold it a kindly deed to heal a leper. But no man shall raise the dead. . . . It would be terrible if the dead came back.

THE VOICE OF IOKANAAN

Ah! The wanton one! The harlot! Ah! the daughter of Babylon with her golden eyes and her gilded eyelids! Thus saith the Lord God, Let there come up against her a multitude of men. Let the people take stones and stone her. . . .

HERODIAS

Command him to be silent!

THE VOICE OF IOKANAAN

Let the captains of the hosts pierce her with their swords, let them crush her beneath their shields.

HERODIAS

Nay, but it is infamous.

THE VOICE OF IOKANAAN

It is thus that I will wipe out all wickedness from the earth, and that all women shall learn not to imitate her abominations.

HERODIAS

You hear what he says against me? You suffer him to revile her who is your wife!

HEROD

He did not speak your name.

HERODIAS

What does that matter? You know well that it is I whom he seeks to revile. And I am your wife, am I not?

HEROD

Of a truth, dear and noble Herodias, you are my wife, and before that you were the wife of my brother.

HERODIAS

It was thou didst snatch me from his arms.

HEROD

Of a truth I was stronger than he was. . . . But let us not talk of that matter. I do not desire to talk of it. It is the cause of the terrible words that the prophet has spoken. Peradventure on account of it a misfortune will come. Let us not speak of this matter. Noble Herodias, we are not mindful of our guests. Fill thou my cup, my well-beloved. Ho! fill with wine the great goblets of silver, and the great goblets of glass. I will drink to Cæsar. There are Romans here, we must drink to Cæsar.

ALL

Cæsar! Cæsar!

HEROD

Do you not see your daughter, how pale she is?

HERODIAS

What is it to you if she be pale or not?

43

HEROD

Never have I seen her so pale.

HERODIAS

You must not look at her.

THE VOICE OF IOKANAAN

In that day the sun shall become black like
sackcloth of hair, and the moon shall become like
blood, and the stars of the heaven shall fall upon
the earth like unripe figs that fall from the fig-
tree, and the kings of the earth shall be afraid.

HERODIAS

Ah! ah! I should like to see that day of which
he speaks, when the moon shall become like
blood, and when the stars shall fall upon the
earth like unripe figs. This prophet talks like a
drunken man, . . . but I cannot suffer the sound
of his voice. I hate his voice. Command him to
be silent.

HEROD

I will not. I cannot understand what it is that
he saith, but it may be an omen.

HERODIAS

I do not believe in omens. He speaks like a
drunken man.

HEROD

It may be he is drunk with the wine of God.

44

HERODIAS

What wine is that, the wine of God? From what vineyards is it gathered? In what wine-press may one find it?

HEROD

[*From this point he looks all the while at Salome.*] Tigellinus, when you were at Rome of late, did the Emperor speak with you on the subject of . . . ?

TIGELLINUS

On what subject, my lord?

HEROD

On what subject? Ah! I asked you a question, did I not? I have forgotten what I would have asked you.

HERODIAS

You are looking again at my daughter. You must not look at her. I have already said so.

HEROD

You say nothing else.

HERODIAS

I say it again.

HEROD

And that restoration of the Temple about which they have talked so much, will anything be done? They say that the veil of the Sanctuary has disappeared, do they not?

45

HERODIAS

It was thyself didst steal it.   Thou speakest at random and without wit.   I will not stay here. Let us go within.

HEROD

Dance for me, Salome.

HERODIAS

I will not have her dance.

SALOME

I have no desire to dance, Tetrarch.

HEROD

Salome, daughter of Herodias, dance for me.

HERODIAS

Peace.   Let her alone.

HEROD

I command thee to dance, Salome.

SALOME

I will not dance, Tetrarch.

HERODIAS

[*Laughing.*]   You see how she obeys you.

HEROD

What is it to me whether she dance or not?

It is nought to me.   To-night I am happy.   I am
exceeding happy.   Never have I been so happy.

FIRST SOLDIER

The Tetrarch has a sombre look.   Has he not
a sombre look ?

SECOND SOLDIER

Yes, he has a sombre look.

HEROD

Wherefore should I not be happy ?   Cæsar, who
is lord of the world, Cæsar, who is lord of all
things, loves me well.   He has just sent me most
precious gifts.   Also he has promised me to
summon to Rome the King of Cappadocia, who is
mine enemy.   It may be that at Rome he will
crucify him, for he is able to do all things that he
has a mind to do.   Verily, Cæsar is lord.   Therefore I do well to be happy.   I am very happy,
never have I been so happy.   There is nothing in
the world that can mar my happiness.

THE VOICE OF IOKANAAN

He shall be seated on his throne.   He shall be
clothed in scarlet and purple.   In his hand he
shall bear a golden cup full of his blasphemies.
And the angel of the Lord shall smite him.   He
shall be eaten of worms.

HERODIAS

You hear what he says about you.   He says
that you shall be eaten of worms.

47

HEROD

It is not of me that he speaks. He speaks
never against me. It is of the King of Cappadocia
that he speaks ; the King of Cappadocia who is
mine enemy. It is he who shall be eaten of
worms. It is not I. Never has he spoken word
against me, this prophet, save that I sinned in
taking to wife the wife of my brother. It may be
he is right. For, of a truth, you are sterile.

HERODIAS

I am sterile, I ? You say that, you that are
ever looking at my daughter, you that would have
her dance for your pleasure? You speak as a
fool. I have borne a child. You have gotten no
child, no, not on one of your slaves. It is you
who are sterile, not I.

HEROD

Peace, woman ! I say that you are sterile. You
have borne me no child, and the prophet says
that our marriage is not a true marriage. He says
that it is a marriage of incest, a marriage that will
bring evils. . . . I fear he is right ; I am sure
that he is right. But it is not the hour to speak
of these things. I would be happy at this moment.
Of a truth, I am happy. There is nothing I lack.

HERODIAS

I am glad you are of so fair a humour to-night.
It is not your custom. But it is late. Let us go

within. Do not forget that we hunt at sunrise. All honours must be shown to Cæsar's ambassadors, must they not?

SECOND SOLDIER

The Tetrarch has a sombre look.

FIRST SOLDIER

Yes, he has a sombre look.

HEROD

Salome, Salome, dance for me. I pray thee dance for me. I am sad to-night. Yes, I am passing sad to-night. When I came hither I slipped in blood, which is an ill omen ; also I heard in the air a beating of wings, a beating of giant wings. I cannot tell what that may mean. . . . I am sad to-night. Therefore dance for me. Dance for me, Salome, I beseech thee. If thou dancest for me thou mayest ask of me what thou wilt, and I will give it thee. Yes, dance for me, Salome, and whatsoever thou shalt ask of me I will give it thee, even unto the half of my kingdom.

SALOME

[*Rising.*] Will you indeed give me whatsoever I shall ask of you, Tetrarch?

HERODIAS

Do not dance, my daughter.

HEROD

Whatsoever thou shalt ask of me, even unto the half of my kingdom.

SALOME

You swear it, Tetrarch ?

HEROD

I swear it, Salome.

HERODIAS

Do not dance, my daughter.

SALOME

By what will you swear this thing, Tetrarch ?

HEROD

By my life, by my crown, by my gods. Whatsoever thou shalt desire I will give it thee, even to the half of my kingdom, if thou wilt but dance for me. O Salome, Salome, dance for me !

SALOME

You have sworn an oath, Tetrarch.

HEROD

I have sworn an oath.

HERODIAS

My daughter, do not dance.

HEROD

Even to the half of my kingdom. Thou wilt be passing fair as a queen, Salome, if it please thee to ask for the half of my kingdom. Will she not be fair as a queen? Ah! it is cold here! There is an icy wind, and I hear . . . wherefore do I hear in the air this beating of wings? Ah! one might fancy a huge black bird that hovers over the terrace. Why can I not see it, this bird? The beat of its wings is terrible. The breath of the wind of its wings is terrible. It is a chill wind. Nay, but it is not cold, it is hot. I am choking. Pour water on my hands. Give me snow to eat. Loosen my mantle. Quick! quick! loosen my mantle. Nay, but leave it. It is my garland that hurts me, my garland of roses. The flowers are like fire. They have burned my forehead. [*He tears the wreath from his head, and throws it on the table.*] Ah! I can breathe now. How red those petals are! They are like stains of blood on the cloth. That does not matter. It is not wise to find symbols in everything that one sees. It makes life too full of terrors. It were better to say that stains of blood are as lovely as rose-petals. It were better far to say that. . . . But we will not speak of this. Now I am happy. I am passing happy. Have I not the right to be happy? Your daughter is going to dance for me. Wilt thou not dance for me, Salome? Thou hast promised to dance for me.

HERODIAS

I will not have her dance.

SALOME

I will dance for you, Tetrarch.

HEROD

You hear what your daughter says. She is going
to dance for me. Thou doest well to dance for me,
Salome. And when thou hast danced for me,
forget not to ask of me whatsoever thou hast a
mind to ask. Whatsoever thou shalt desire I will
give it thee, even to the half of my kingdom. I
have sworn it, have I not?

SALOME

Thou hast sworn it, Tetrarch.

HEROD

And I have never failed of my word. I am not
of those who break their oaths. I know not how
to lie. I am the slave of my word, and my word
is the word of a king. The King of Cappadocia
had ever a lying tongue, but he is no true king.
He is a coward. Also he owes me money that he
will not repay. He has even insulted my ambassadors. He has spoken words that were wound-
ing. But Cæsar will crucify him when he comes
to Rome. I know that Cæsar will crucify him.
And if he crucify him not, yet will he die, being
eaten of worms. The prophet has prophesied it.
Well! Wherefore dost thou tarry, Salome?

SALOME

I am waiting until my slaves bring perfumes to
me and the seven veils, and take from off my feet
my sandals. [*Slaves bring perfumes and the seven
veils, and take off the sandals of Salome.*]

52

HEROD

Ah, thou art to dance with naked feet! 'Tis well! 'Tis well! Thy little feet will be like white doves. They will be like little white flowers that dance upon the trees. . . . No, no, she is going to dance on blood! There is blood spilt on the ground. She must not dance on blood. It were an evil omen.

HERODIAS

What is it to thee if she dance on blood? Thou hast waded deep enough in it. . . .

HEROD

What is it to me? Ah! look at the moon! She has become red. She has become red as blood. Ah! the prophet prophesied truly. He prophesied that the moon would become as blood. Did he not prophesy it? All of ye heard him prophesying it. And now the moon has become as blood. Do ye not see it?

HERODIAS

Oh yes, I see it well, and the stars are falling like unripe figs, are they not? and the sun is becoming black like sackcloth of hair, and the kings of the earth are afraid. That at least one can see. The prophet is justified of his words in that at least, for truly the kings of the earth are afraid. . . . Let us go within. You are sick. They will say at Rome that you are mad. Let us go within, I tell you.

53

THE VOICE OF IOKANAAN

Who is this who cometh from Edom, who is this who cometh from Bozra, whose raiment is dyed with purple, who shineth in the beauty of his garments, who walketh mighty in his greatness? Wherefore is thy raiment stained with scarlet?

HERODIAS

Let us go within. The voice of that man maddens me. I will not have my daughter dance while he is continually crying out. I will not have her dance while you look at her in this fashion. In a word, I will not have her dance.

HEROD

Do not rise, my wife, my queen, it will avail thee nothing. I will not go within till she hath danced. Dance, Salome, dance for me.

HERODIAS

Do not dance, my daughter.

SALOME

I am ready, Tetrarch.
[*Salome dances the dance of the seven veils.*]

HEROD

Ah! wonderful! wonderful! You see that she has danced for me, your daughter. Come near, Salome, come near, that I may give thee thy fee. Ah! I pay a royal price to those who dance for my pleasure. I will pay thee royally. I will give thee whatsoever thy soul desireth. What wouldst thou have? Speak.

SALOME

[*Kneeling.*] I would that they presently bring me in a silver charger . . .

HEROD

[*Laughing.*] In a silver charger? Surely yes, in a silver charger. She is charming, is she not? What is it that thou wouldst have in a silver charger, O sweet and fair Salome, thou that art fairer than all the daughters of Judæa? What wouldst thou have them bring thee in a silver charger? Tell me. Whatsoever it may be, thou shalt receive it. My treasures belong to thee. What is it that thou wouldst have, Salome?

SALOME

[*Rising.*] The head of Iokanaan.

HERODIAS

Ah! that is well said, my daughter.

HEROD

No, no!

HERODIAS

That is well said, my daughter.

HEROD

No, no, Salome. It is not that thou desirest.
Do not listen to thy mother's voice. She is ever
giving thee evil counsel. Do not heed her.

SALOME

It is not my mother's voice that I heed. It is for
mine own pleasure that I ask the head of Iokanaan
in a silver charger. You have sworn an oath,
Herod. Forget not that you have sworn an oath.

HEROD

I know it. I have sworn an oath by my gods.
I know it well. But I pray thee, Salome, ask of
me something else. Ask of me the half of my
kingdom, and I will give it thee. But ask not of
me what thy lips have asked.

SALOME

I ask of you the head of Iokanaan.

HEROD

No, no, I will not give it thee.

SALOME

You have sworn an oath, Herod.

HERODIAS

Yes, you have sworn an oath. Everybody heard
you. You swore it before everybody.

HEROD

Peace, woman! It is not to you I speak.

HERODIAS

My daughter has done well to ask the head of
Iokanaan. He has covered me with insults. He
has said unspeakable things against me. One can
see that she loves her mother well. Do not yield,
my daughter. He has sworn an oath, he has
sworn an oath.

HEROD

Peace! Speak not to me! . . . Salome, I pray
thee be not stubborn. I have ever been kind
toward thee. I have ever loved thee. . . . It may
be that I have loved thee too much. Therefore
ask not this thing of me. This is a terrible thing,
an awful thing to ask of me. Surely, I think thou
art jesting. The head of a man that is cut from
his body is ill to look upon, is it not? It is not
meet that the eyes of a virgin should look upon
such a thing. What pleasure couldst thou have
in it. There is no pleasure that thou couldst have
in it. No, no, it is not that thou desirest. Hearken
to me. I have an emerald, a great emerald and
round, that the minion of Cæsar has sent unto me.
When thou lookest through this emerald thou
canst see that which passeth afar off. Cæsar himself carries such an emerald when he goes to the
circus. But my emerald is the larger. I know
well that it is the larger. It is the largest emerald
in the whole world. Thou wilt take that, wilt thou
not? Ask it of me and I will give it thee.

SALOME

I demand the head of Iokanaan.

HEROD

Thou art not listening. Thou art not listening
Suffer me to speak, Salome.

SALOME

The head of Iokanaan!

HEROD

No, no, thou wouldst not have that. Thou
sayest that but to trouble me, because that I have
looked at thee and ceased not this night. It is
true, I have looked at thee and ceased not this
night. Thy beauty has troubled me. Thy beauty
has grievously troubled me, and I have looked at
thee overmuch. Nay, but I will look at thee no
more. One should not look at anything. Neither
at things, nor at people should one look. Only in
mirrors is it well to look, for mirrors do but show us
masks. Oh! oh! bring wine! I thirst. . . . Salome,
Salome, let us be as friends. Bethink thee. . . .
Ah! what would I say? What was 't? Ah! I remember it! . . . Salome,—nay but come nearer to
me ; I fear thou wilt not hear my words,—Salome,
thou knowest my white peacocks, my beautiful
white peacocks, that walk in the garden between
the myrtles and the tall cypress-trees. Their
beaks are gilded with gold and the grains that
they eat are smeared with gold, and their feet are
stained with purple. When they cry out the rain
comes, and the moon shows herself in the heavens
when they spread their tails. Two by two they
walk between the cypress-trees and the black

58

myrtles, and each has a slave to tend it. Sometimes they fly across the trees, and anon they
couch in the grass, and round the pools of the
water. There are not in all the world birds so
wonderful. I know that Cæsar himself has no
birds so fair as my birds. I will give thee fifty of
my peacocks. They will follow thee whither-
soever thou goest, and in the midst of them thou
wilt be like unto the moon in the midst of a
great white cloud. . . . I will give them to thee, all.
I have but a hundred, and in the whole world
there is no king who has peacocks like unto my
peacocks. But I will give them all to thee. Only
thou must loose me from my oath, and must not
ask of me that which thy lips have asked of me.
              [*He empties the cup of wine.*]

SALOME

Give me the head of Iokanaan!

HERODIAS

Well said, my daughter! As for you, you are
ridiculous with your peacocks.

HEROD

Peace! you are always crying out. You cry
out like a beast of prey. You must not cry in such
fashion. Your voice wearies me. Peace, I tell you!
. . . Salome, think on what thou art doing. It may
be that this man comes from God. He is a holy
man. The finger of God has touched him. God

59

has put terrible words into his mouth. In the palace, as in the desert, God is ever with him. . . . It may be that He is, at least. One cannot tell, but it is possible that God is with him and for him. If he die also, peradventure some evil may befall me. Verily, he has said that evil will befall some one on the day whereon he dies. On whom should it fall if it fall not on me? Remember, I slipped in blood when I came hither. Also did I not hear a beating of wings in the air, a beating of vast wings? These are ill omens. And there were other things. I am sure that there were other things, though I saw them not. Thou wouldst not that some evil should befall me, Salome? Listen to me again.

SALOME

Give me the head of Iokanaan!

HEROD

Ah! thou art not listening to me. Be calm. As for me, am I not calm? I am altogether calm. Listen. I have jewels hidden in this place —jewels that thy mother even has never seen; jewels that are marvellous to look at. I have a collar of pearls, set in four rows. They are like unto moons chained with rays of silver. They are even as half a hundred moons caught in a golden net. On the ivory breast of a queen they have rested. Thou shalt be as fair as a queen when thou wearest them. I have amethysts of two kinds; one that is black like wine, and one that is red like wine that one has coloured with water. I have topazes yellow as are the eyes of tigers, and topazes that are pink as the eyes of a wood-pigeon, and green topazes that are as the eyes of cats. I have opals that burn always, with a flame that is cold as ice, opals that make sad men's minds, and are afraid of the shadows. I have onyxes like the eyeballs of a dead woman. I have moonstones that change when the moon changes, and are wan when they see the sun. I have sapphires big like eggs, and as blue as blue flowers. The sea wanders within them, and the moon comes never to trouble the blue of their waves. I have chrysolites and beryls, and chrysoprases and rubies; I have sardonyx and hyacinth stones, and stones of chalcedony, and I will give them all unto thee, all, and other things will I add to them. The King of the Indies has but even now sent me four fans fashioned from the feathers of parrots, and the King of Numidia a garment of ostrich feathers. I have a crystal, into which it is not lawful for a woman to look, nor may young men behold it until they have been beaten with rods. In a coffer of nacre I have three wondrous turquoises. He who wears them on his forehead can imagine things which are not, and he who carries them in his hand can turn the fruitful woman into a woman that is barren. These are great treasures. They are treasures above all price. But this is not all. In an ebony coffer I have two cups of amber that are like apples of pure gold. If an enemy pour poison into these cups they become like apples of silver. In a coffer incrusted with amber I have

sandals incrusted with glass. I have mantles that
have been brought from the land of the Seres, and
bracelets decked about with carbuncles and with
jade that come from the city of Euphrates. . . .
What desirest thou more than this, Salome? Tell
me the thing that thou desirest, and I will give it
thee. All that thou askest I will give thee, save
one thing only. I will give thee all that is mine,
save only the life of one man. I will give thee
the mantle of the high priest. I will give thee
the veil of the sanctuary.

THE JEWS

Oh! oh!

SALOME

Give me the head of Iokanaan!

HEROD

[*Sinking back in his seat.*] Let her be given
what she asks! Of a truth she is her mother's
child! [*The first Soldier approaches. Herodias
draws from the hand of the Tetrarch the ring of
death, and gives it to the Soldier, who straightway
bears it to the Executioner. The Executioner looks
scared.*] Who has taken my ring? There was a
ring on my right hand. Who has drunk my wine?
There was wine in my cup. It was full of wine.
Some one has drunk it! Oh! surely some evil
will befall some one. [*The Executioner goes down
into the cistern.*] Ah! wherefore did I give my

oath? Hereafter let no king swear an oath. If
he keep it not, it is terrible, and if he keep it, it is
terrible also.

HERODIAS

My daughter has done well.

HEROD

I am sure that some misfortune will happen.

SALOME

[*She leans over the cistern and listens.*] There
is no sound. I hear nothing. Why does he not
cry out, this man? Ah! if any man sought to
kill me, I would cry out, I would struggle, I would
not suffer. . . . Strike, strike, Naaman, strike, I
tell you. . . . No, I hear nothing. There is a
silence, a terrible silence. Ah! something has
fallen upon the ground. I heard something fall.
It was the sword of the executioner. He is afraid,
this slave. He has dropped his sword. He dares
not kill him. He is a coward, this slave! Let
soldiers be sent. [*She sees the Page of Herodias
and addresses him.*] Come hither. Thou wert
the friend of him who is dead, wert thou not?
Well, I tell thee, there are not dead men enough.
Go to the soldiers and bid them go down and
bring me the thing I ask, the thing the Tetrarch
has promised me, the thing that is mine. [*The
Page recoils. She turns to the soldiers*] Hither, ye
soldiers. Get ye down into this cistern and
bring me the head of this man. Tetrarch, Tetrarch,

63

command your soldiers that they bring me the head of Iokanaan.

[*A huge black arm, the arm of the Executioner, comes forth from the cistern, bearing on a silver shield the head of Iokanaan. Salome seizes it. Herod hides his face with his cloak. Herodias smiles and fans herself. The Nazarenes fall on their knees and begin to pray.*]

Ah! thou wouldst not suffer me to kiss thy mouth, Iokanaan. Well! I will kiss it now. I will bite it with my teeth as one bites a ripe fruit. Yes, I will kiss thy mouth, Iokanaan. I said it; did I not say it? I said it. Ah! I will kiss it now. . . . But wherefore dost thou not look at me, Iokanaan? Thine eyes that were so terrible, so full of rage and scorn, are shut now. Wherefore are they shut? Open thine eyes! Lift up thine eyelids, Iokanaan! Wherefore dost thou not look at me? Art thou afraid of me, Iokanaan, that thou wilt not look at me? . . . And thy tongue, that was like a red snake darting poison, it moves no more, it speaks no words, Iokanaan, that scarlet viper that spat its venom upon me. It is strange, is it not? How is it that the red viper stirs no longer? . . . Thou wouldst have none of me, Iokanaan. Thou rejectedst me. Thou didst speak evil words against me. Thou didst bear thyself toward me as to a harlot, as to a woman that is a wanton, to me, Salome, daughter of Herodias, Princess of Judæa! Well, I still live, but thou art dead, and thy head belongs to me. I can do with it what I will. I can throw it to the dogs and to the birds of the air. That which the dogs leave, the birds of the air shall devour. . . . Ah, Iokanaan, Iokanaan, thou wert the man that I loved alone among men! All other men were hateful to me. But thou wert beautiful! Thy body was a column of ivory set upon feet of silver. It was a garden full of doves and lilies of silver. It was a tower of silver decked with shields of ivory. There was nothing in the world so white as thy body. There was nothing in the world so black as thy hair. In the whole world there was nothing so red as thy mouth. Thy voice was a censer that scattered strange perfumes, and when I looked on thee I heard a strange music. Ah! wherefore didst thou not look at me, Iokanaan? With the cloak of thine hands, and with the cloak of thy blasphemies thou didst hide thy face. Thou didst put upon thine eyes the covering of him who would see his God. Well, thou hast seen thy God, Iokanaan, but me, me, thou didst never see. If thou hadst seen me thou hadst loved me. I saw thee, and I loved thee. Oh, how I loved thee! I love thee yet, Iokanaan. I love only thee. . . . I am athirst for thy beauty; I am hungry for thy body; and neither wine nor apples can appease my desire. What shall I do now, Iokanaan? Neither the floods nor the great waters can quench my passion. I was a princess, and thou didst scorn me. I was a virgin, and thou didst take my virginity from me. I was chaste, and thou didst fill my veins with fire. . . . Ah! ah! wherefore didst thou not look at me? If thou hadst looked at me thou hadst loved me. Well I know that thou wouldst have loved me, and

the mystery of Love is greater than the mystery
of Death.

HEROD

She is monstrous, thy daughter; I tell thee she
is monstrous. In truth, what she has done is a
great crime. I am sure that it is a crime against
some unknown God.

HERODIAS

I am well pleased with my daughter. She has
done well. And I would stay here now.

HEROD

[*Rising*]. Ah! There speaks my brother's
wife! Come! I will not stay in this place. Come,
I tell thee. Surely some terrible thing will befall.
Manasseh, Issachar, Ozias, put out the torches. I
will not look at things, I will not suffer things to
look at me. Put out the torches! Hide the moon!
Hide the stars! Let us hide ourselves in our
palace, Herodias. I begin to be afraid.
[*The slaves put out the torches. The stars disap-
pear. A great cloud crosses the moon and conceals it
completely. The stage becomes quite dark. The
Tetrarch begins to climb the staircase.*]

THE VOICE OF SALOME

Ah! I have kissed thy mouth, Iokanaan, I
have kissed thy mouth. There was a bitter taste
on thy lips. Was it the taste of blood? . . . Nay;
but perchance it was the taste of love. . . . They

say that love hath a bitter taste. . . . But what matter? what matter? I have kissed thy mouth, Iokanaan, I have kissed thy mouth.

[*A ray of moonlight falls on Salome and illumines her.*]

HEROD

[*Turning round and seeing Salome.*]   Kill that woman!

[*The soldiers rush forward and crush beneath their shields Salome, daughter of Herodias, Princess of Judæa.*]

CURTAIN.

A SELECTION OF ILLUSTRATIONS

By Aubrey Beardsley